STANLEY YELNATS' SURVIVAL GUIDE TO CAMP GREEN LAKE

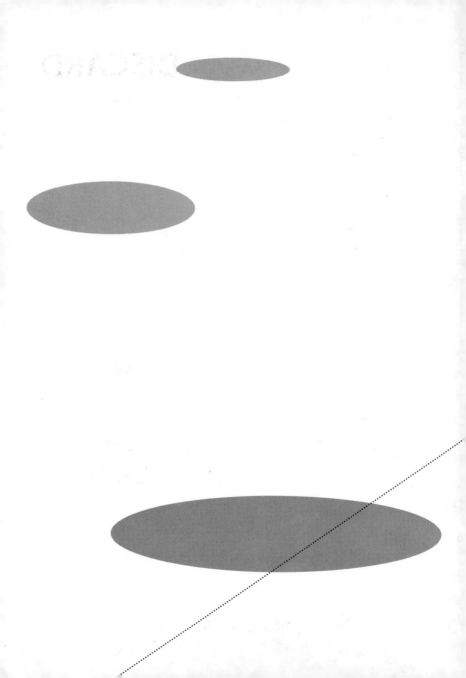

Stanley Yelnats'
SURVIVAL
GUIDE

TO CAMP GREEN LAKE

BY LOUIS SACHAR

A Dell Yearling Book

Published by
Dell Yearling
an imprint of
Random House Children's Books
a division of Random House, Inc.
New York

Visit us on the Web! www.randomhouse.com/kids

Educators and librarians, for a variety of teaching tools,
visit us at www.randomhouse.com/teachers

ISBN: 0-440-41947-6

Printed in the United States of America

March 2003

10 9 8 7 6 5 4

CWO

Contents

1

If I Can Do It, So Can You

If you're reading this book, chances are you've been convicted of a crime and have been sentenced to the Camp Green Lake Juvenile Correctional Facility or someplace similar. Maybe you're innocent—more likely not.

You're probably scared. If you're not scared, you're in big trouble. Fear keeps you alert. But don't give in to your fear. You can't let it cloud your mind. You don't want to be so overcome with fear that you can't think straight.

You probably feel all alone. You are. There are six counselors and thirty-four other campers at Green Lake, but you are still alone. Nobody cares about you. Nobody is interested in making your life better.

Don't go looking for friends. You have to let friendships develop very slowly. You don't know who the other campers are or what crimes they committed.

The guards, or counselors, as they like to be called, are not there to protect you. They are there to see that the routine is not disturbed. If another camper punches you in the face and breaks your nose, you will get in trouble for having a broken nose.

Don't get me wrong. Most of the other boys are not bad guys. In most cases, they just made some bad choices. Maybe they just hung out with the wrong crowd and ended up in a no-win situation. You don't know, and you don't ask. If you're going to survive Camp Green Lake, one of the first things you have to learn is not to ask too many questions.

From here on in, you cannot afford to make any more bad choices. You can't even let anyone else tell you what your choices are. You have to figure that out for yourself.

Look, I'm not a tough guy. In fact, I'm probably the last guy in the world you'd expect to be able to survive Camp Green Lake. My name is Stanley Yelnats. Before I was sent to Camp Green Lake, you might say I was a total loser. (Everyone else said it, why not you?) At school, kids half my size used to pick on me. I had no friends. I was overweight. Everything in life seemed to conspire against me.

If you want, you can read about what happened to me in a book called *Holes*. But this is not about me anymore. It's about you now. And I don't care how mean and tough you are, remember this: There's always somebody meaner and tougher than you are. And one of these days, you're going to find him.

Even more dangerous than the mean, tough guys are the ones who are crazy. You never know what's going to set them off or what they're liable to

do. There was a kid in C tent who ripped apart a mattress because somebody put his hat on the bed.

It's not about being tough. It's about being smart. It's about staying alert. If I can do it, so can you.

2

How the System Works

Camp Green Lake is located in a giant dried-up lake bed deep in the heart of Texas. When I was there, it hadn't rained for over a hundred years. It rained the day I was released, but it is still very hot and very dry.

The camp closed shortly after I left, and I thought that was the end of it. But then *Holes* was published, and lots of law enforcement officials and politicians read it.

They all thought, "Wow, what a great idea!" And they reopened Camp Green Lake. That is why I decided to write this survival guide.

When I was at Camp Green Lake, it was only for boys. Now there is a sister camp about a hundred miles away exclusively for girls. While I can only tell you about Camp Green Lake, I hope my lessons and survival tips will help you at whichever institution you are attending.

The Warden is still the boss of Camp Green Lake. She owns all the land. She speaks in a gentle voice, but don't be fooled. She's as mean as a rattle-

snake. She comes from what was once a very promi-
nent and wealthy family. The family fortune was
wiped out during the hundred-year drought, but she
still has a few connections in the state legislature in
Austin. She used those connections to establish the
Camp Green Lake Juvenile Correctional Facility. Its
mission was to turn bad boys into good boys
through hard work and discipline. The State pays
her to run the facility.

The idea was this: Digging holes builds character.
But here's the first thing you need to understand. The
Warden doesn't care about your character. It's just

HOW THE SYSTEM WORKS

about digging holes. She's obsessed. Every day, you will dig a hole five feet deep and five feet in diameter. As long as you dig your hole, the Warden will leave you alone.

Mr. Sir is the head counselor. He seems like he belongs in prison, instead of being in charge of one. Mr. Pendanski is the counselor of D tent, where I stayed. He will try to be your friend. He's not. In many ways, he's worse than Mr. Sir. At least Mr. Sir doesn't pretend to be something he's not. Mr. Sir acts tough, and Mr. Pendanski pretends to be understanding, but really they both have the same objective: to keep everyone in line; to keep everyone digging their holes.

You will be fed three meals a day, because you need energy to dig holes. Water will be brought out to the holes every two hours. Why? So you can keep digging. You are given time off for relaxation so your body will have the strength to dig another hole.

Don't expect too much in the way of food or water, or entertainment. Remember that any money the Warden doesn't have to spend on you, she gets to keep for herself.

3

Don't Complain

What's the matter? It's too hot? You're tired of digging? Your muscles ache? Your hands have blisters? Your feet have blisters? Your blisters have blisters? The shovels are too long? The showers are too short? Your cot is hard and lumpy? The food is hard and lumpy?

Well, guess what? Everyone else has been there longer than you have. They were sleeping on their hard, lumpy cots, getting up at four-thirty in the morning, and digging five-foot holes under a blazing sun while you were lying on a couch, watching cartoons, and eating Froot Loops. No one wants to hear your complaints. No one likes a whiner.

After a while your hands will harden. Your muscles will harden. Your head will harden. Your soul will harden.

Everyone suffers equally. You're all in this together. Race, skin color, the grades you got at school, whether you were one of the popular kids; none of that matters. You will earn the respect of the others by doing your job without grumbling. No it's-not-fair's. No I-don't-belong-here's. But don't go overboard the other way, either. You don't want to wake up every morning singing "Zip-A-Dee-Doo-Dah."

SURVIVAL TEST

1

You have finished digging your hole and are returning to the camp compound when you hear a rattling noise. You look down to see a large snake coiled in front of you. Its forked tongue darts in and out between two large fangs as its cold eyes stare at you. You should:

A: Say, "It isn't fair. This question comes after section three, and the part on rattlesnakes isn't until section ten."

B: Carefully study the snake, making note of its markings and the shape of its head. Measure its width and length. This is important because when you report it to the proper authorities, you will know what you are talking about and won't sound like a blubbering idiot.

C: Hit it with your shovel, or, better yet, put down your shovel and fight it bare-handed. After all, you're the meanest and toughest kid at Camp Green Lake, and no overgrown worm is going to disrespect you!

D: Pretend it isn't there and just keep walking as you whistle "Zip-A-Dee-Doo-Dah."

E: Try to make friends with the snake, and explain in a soothing voice that you have no intention of harming it. Gently pat its head as you tell it that even though you are a criminal, you have a good heart.

ANSWER

A is incorrect. While at Camp Green Lake, you will have to make all kinds of life-or-death decisions, ready or not.

B is incorrect. There are no proper authorities at Camp Green Lake.

C is incorrect. There is always someone meaner and tougher than you are.

D is incorrect. You can pretend the snake isn't there, but the snake will not pretend you're not there. You will not survive Camp Green Lake by ignoring danger.

E is incorrect. This isn't a Disney movie.

The correct answer is Q, as in: Quickly, get away from the snake. Walk, don't run.

This wasn't really a test on rattlesnakes. It was a test on making choices. You can't let anybody else tell you what your choices are. Sometimes they won't give you the right choice. If you're going to survive Camp Green Lake, you must always make the right choice, whether it's given to you or not.

In fact, sometimes it's best not to answer anyone's questions. Zero knew that. He was a kid in D tent who hardly spoke, so a lot of people thought he was stupid. Zero wasn't stupid. He only spoke when he wanted to say something.

Do you remember what the police officer said to you when you were arrested? You have the right to remain silent. Most people talk way too much.

4

Armpit's Suggestion

Mr. Pendanski keeps a suggestion box just outside the office door. A pencil hangs on a string, and there's a pad of paper. On each sheet of paper is a place to put your name, your tent, and your suggestion.

"We're all looking for ways we can improve," he told us. "You, me, the Warden. We're all in this together, and if anybody has any ideas that could have a positive effect on our lives, it will be greatly appreciated."

Most of the sugges-
tions were what you'd

expect, and I can't repeat them here. Other suggestions just had no chance. "Get pizza delivered for
dinner." Even if pizza didn't cost too much, the nearest pizza parlor was over a hundred miles away.
"Friday-night dances with a Girl Scout camp." As if
parents would let their daughters hang out with us.
"Why don't the counselors dig one day a week, to
see what it's like?" Yeah, right.

Squid once wrote, "Get a pencil that doesn't
break." Then he broke the pencil. Somehow, he got
caught and had to wash pots and pans for a week.

A lot of the guys believed that the Warden
watched us on hidden cameras, so she might have
seen Squid break the pencil. I don't think so. I don't
think the Warden cares about Mr. Pendanski's pencil.

I once made a suggestion. It was a way to save
paper. "Get rid of the suggestion box." I didn't give
my name.

Magnet once wrote: "How about letting us listen
to music while we dig?" He even signed his name.
"Magnet, D tent." He thought it would be a good
idea because the rhythm might help us dig faster,
but Mr. Pendanski never even commented on it.

"He never even reads the suggestions," X-Ray insisted. "It's just a way to let the campers blow off steam."

But then Armpit came up with a suggestion. You could tell he'd been thinking about it a long time, which surprised me because I'd never realized Armpit thought about much. It had to do with the showers.

Water was very scarce. It was expensive to bring water into Camp Green Lake. We were allowed only a four-minute shower every day. After four minutes, the shower shut off automatically.

Those four minutes were the best part of the day. Four minutes of heaven in a day of hell. The water wasn't artificially heated, but with the sun beating down on it all day, it was just warm enough to be comfortable.

"I was thinking about putting a suggestion in Mom's suggestion box," Armpit said.

In case you haven't noticed, we all had nicknames. I was Caveman. Mom was our nickname for Mr. Pendanski.

It was about eight-thirty at night. We were all lying in our cots, but no one was asleep yet.

"This I gotta hear," said Squid.

"Wouldn't it be better if we could break up our shower time?" asked Armpit.

"What are you talking about?" asked X-Ray.

"You waste water when you put on soap," Armpit said. "What if the water only went for forty-five seconds, then turned off? Just long enough to get you wet all over. Then you could take as much time as you need to get the soap on. Then turn the water back on for three minutes and fifteen seconds."

He'd even done the math.

"So what do you think?" he asked. "It's still a four-minute shower, so it doesn't use any more water. But we get to enjoy it for a longer time."

I was surprised. It really did make sense.

For a moment nobody said anything. We just stared at him.

"You amaze me, Armpit," X-Ray finally said. "Brains, *and* good looks."

Armpit didn't know if X-Ray was making fun of him.

"That's really smart!" said Zigzag.

"We'd get cleaner, too," said Squid, " 'cause some-times I don't have time to get the soap all over me."

"Yeah, I've noticed," said Magnet, holding his nose.

"What do you think, Caveman?" Armpit asked me. He knew I'd give him a straight answer.

"I think it's a really great idea, Armpit," I told him.

Once he realized we weren't making fun of him, Armpit beamed a great big smile.

We all helped Armpit put his suggestion down on paper. There was a lot of discussion on how much time it takes to get wet, and to put soap on, but we decided the simpler, the better. This is what we finally came up with.

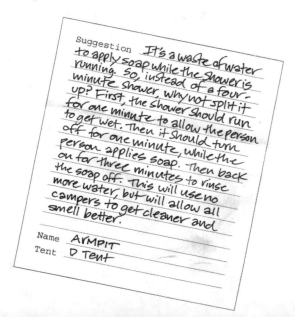

Suggestion It's a waste of water to apply soap while the shower is running. So, instead of a four-minute shower, why not split it up? First, the shower should run for one minute to allow the person to get wet. Then it should turn off for one minute, while the person applies soap. Then back on for three minutes to rinse the soap off. This will use no more water, but will allow all campers to get cleaner and smell better.

Name   ARMPIT
Tent   D Tent

We all watched Armpit proudly sign his name and drop the suggestion in the box. Three days later I saw Mr. Sir working on the showers.

The guys from D tent gathered around. X-Ray asked, "Whatcha doin', Mr. Sir?"

"Adjusting the mechanism," Mr. Sir replied. "So that the showers can stop and start."

Magnet patted Armpit on the back.

That evening after dinner, Mr. Pendanski stood up and made an announcement.

"There will be a change in the shower procedure," he said. "It is a waste of water to apply soap while the shower is running. Don't worry. The showers will still last four minutes. But first they will run for one minute to allow you to get wet. Then the shower will shut off and remain off for exactly one minute. During that time you will apply the soap. Then the shower will come back on for the remaining two minutes. This will give you plenty of time to rinse off the soap. Remember, a clean body is a healthy body."

I couldn't believe it. Maybe I hadn't heard right.

"Did Mom just say *two minutes*?" asked Armpit.

I'd heard correctly. We still had a four-minute shower, but only three minutes of water.

"Great idea, Armpit," grumbled Zigzag.

"Do us all a favor, Armpit," said X-Ray, "and don't get any more smart ideas."

Squid told Armpit where to stick his next suggestion, and it wasn't in the suggestion box.

They didn't have to worry. Armpit didn't get any more ideas. At least, none that he told us.

The suggestion box isn't about making your life better. It's about making the Warden's life better. Thanks to Armpit's suggestion, the Warden was able to save water.

5

Scorpions

I should warn you. My knowledge of scorpions and the other wildlife at Camp Green Lake is based on my personal observations and is not scientific. I came across two types of scorpions at Camp Green Lake: big ones and little ones. Actually, they came across me.

Habitat: Scorpions live in shoes, hats, sheets, pillows, and piles of old clothes. It makes you wonder how they survived before people came along.

Always check each article of clothing before

getting dressed, whether in the tent or after you shower. Always check your bed and pillow before lying down.

How to recognize a scorpion: They are really ugly. The good thing about scorpions is that they are so ugly, you can't help jumping back when you see one. But don't scream. It's never a good idea to scream at Camp Green Lake.

The big ones are about four inches long, an inch wide, and a fourth of an inch thick. The little ones are about an inch and a half long, and the rest of their measurements are proportional to that.

Scorpions have two claws, six very skinny legs, and a segmented tail. They have no face, so it is difficult to tell one scorpion from another.

The legs: Scorpion legs are extremely skinny and are capable of very quick movement, but you don't have to worry about being chased by a scorpion. They would be very fast runners, but fortunately they're not smart enough to get their legs to work together. It's like each leg doesn't know what the other legs are doing. The legs go in different directions at different speeds, so mostly they just move around in uneven loops.

The danger is that one might randomly wander across your face while you are sleeping. Since they don't have faces themselves, they don't know what one is, and it scares them. Like all living creatures, including humans, scorpions are most dangerous when they are frightened.

The claws: Their claws look like tiny crab claws. Getting pinched by a scorpion claw is no worse than, say, getting pinched by someone at school because you didn't wear green on St. Patrick's Day, except when you get pinched by someone at school, you don't expect him to suddenly swing his butt around and inject you with poison.

The tail: The tail is the most dangerous part of the scorpion. It is divided into six segments, with a stinger at the very tip. You might think you're safe if you stay in front of a scorpion, but before you know it, it can whip its tail around to the front. This rapid movement is possible because it has no face to get in the way.

6

Zigzag's *TV Guide*

Each camper is given a crate for keeping personal items in: toothbrush, toothpaste, towels, etc. Whatever you put in there, everybody will know what you have. The crates are open. There are no lids, let alone locks. But no one will touch your stuff. It's an unwritten law, like no throwing dirt in someone else's hole.

Each guy usually has something else in his crate, too, what I call a lifeline. It's something that connects him to life back home. I

When picking up a scorpion, you should grab it by its tail, holding on to the segment right next to the stinger.

What to do if you are stung by a scorpion: Usually the worst thing about a scorpion sting is just how bad it hurts. The pain is excruciating. It feels like your skin is being ripped off your bones. The pain will slowly spread to your joints and muscles. That was how Armpit got his name. He got stung on the arm and later went on and on about how much his armpit hurt.

Sometimes a scorpion sting can result in sickness and a high fever. Barf Bag lost his breakfast after he got bitten on the finger, but that might have had more to do with the breakfast than with the scorpion.

There was a kid in E tent who lost all feeling in his face for three hours after getting stung on the neck. He had trouble breathing. That was the only time anyone came close to dying at Camp Green Lake from a scorpion sting.

The best thing you can do is wash the area with soap and water so it doesn't get infected and wait for the pain to go away. You will have a very red, and very sore, welt for a week or two.

SCORPIONS

SURVIVAL TEST

2

It is an oppressively hot day. (What else is new?) You've been digging your hole for several hours. You reach down and pick up your canteen, then notice a dark spot on the ground. To your horror, you realize there's a tiny hole in the bottom of your canteen. Only half your water is left. You should:

A: Get mad and smash your canteen with your shovel, causing more and bigger leaks.

B: Quickly guzzle the remaining water in your canteen.

C: Be thankful for what you have. Your canteen is not half empty. It is half full.

D: Turn your canteen upside down, so that the small hole is on top. Whenever you want a drink, you won't unscrew the lid, but simply drink out of the hole. The only time you will ever unscrew the lid is when filling the canteen, during which time you will keep your finger over the hole.

E: Ask your counselor for a new canteen.

ANSWER

E is incorrect. If you ask your counselor for a new canteen, he will tell you it's just a small leak. Be thankful for what you have. Your canteen is not half empty. It is half full. He will suggest that you turn your canteen upside down, so that you keep the leak on top.

D is incorrect. Dirt will get into your canteen, and some water will leak out despite your best efforts. You don't want to spend the next eighteen months drinking dirty water out of a leaky canteen.

C is incorrect. While it is important to have a positive attitude, you also need water.

The correct answer is B, then A. First guzzle the remaining water, then smash up your canteen. The Warden knows you cannot dig your holes without water. You will be given a new canteen.

kept a photograph of my parents. Armpit had a catcher's mitt. Squid kept a rubber octopus. Don't ask me why. You don't ask too many questions, and you don't ever cut someone's lifeline.

Zigzag's lifeline was a *TV Guide* dated March 22, 1998. The torn cover showed the crew from one of the *Star Trek* shows. Maybe Zigzag was a Trekkie. A lot of people thought Zigzag was from outer space.

I'd often see Zigzag lying on his cot, carefully studying the pages. He could probably tell you when any show was on that particular week and what was going to happen in it. Of course, whatever was *going to happen* had *already happened.* For most of us, the week of March 22, 1998, was history. For Zigzag, the week ran on a continuous loop.

There was a television inside the Wreck Room, and I guess it's still there. It doesn't come close to working. Even if it did, I doubt there would be any reception. The Warden has a satellite dish outside her cabin, but she lives in a different reality.

Still, every day after digging and showering, Zigzag plopped himself down on the Wreck Room floor and stared at the TV. Whatever he was watching was playing only inside his head, something from the week of March 22, 1998.

It was an old-fashioned TV with one of those big circular knobs used for changing channels. It must have been made before cable, because as far as I could tell, there were only thirteen possible channels.

Sometimes X-Ray would ask, "Hey, Zig. Whatcha watchin'?" and Zigzag would reply, *"I Dream of Jeannie,"* or *"The Simpsons,"* or whatever. No one laughed. No one ever pointed out that there was nothing on the screen. Let sleeping dogs lie. Don't cut someone's lifeline, especially someone as crazy as Zigzag.

Then one day a guy from E tent came over and sat down next to Zigzag. His name was Easy. His real name was Eric Zornlitch. He was called Easy because of his initials.

He was anything but

easygoing. He had been sent to Camp Green Lake in the first place because a dog pooped in front of him when he was riding his skateboard. Easy beat up the dog's owner, and then the dog.

Easy sat down next to Zigzag and stared at the TV. When Zigzag didn't seem to notice him, Easy laughed loudly, as if he was watching something really funny. He slapped Zigzag on the back.

Zigzag looked a little annoyed but otherwise continued to ignore him.

Easy elbowed Zigzag in the side and said, "That was pretty funny, huh?"

Zigzag never laughed or showed any reaction to any show he was watching. He just stared.

Finally, Easy reached over and changed the channel. By this time everybody in the Wreck Room was watching them watch TV. I was beginning to get worried.

Zigzag turned the knob back. "I was here first," he said.

Easy looked over at his friends from E tent and smiled. "But I've seen this show before," he said, and turned the knob again.

"I haven't," said Zigzag. He turned it back.

Some of the other guys in the room began to get into it. "Zigzag's always hogging the set!" someone shouted.

"Let someone else watch something for a change," someone else put in.

Other guys came in on Zigzag's side. "Zigzag was there first. Let him finish his show!"

Easy reached for the channel knob.

Zigzag's hand clamped on top of Easy's. In a dangerously quiet voice he said, "Wait until the show's over."

Zigzag did not seem especially threatening. He resembled a tall, skinny bobblehead doll. But Easy had been around long enough to know that the crazy guys were the most dangerous.

Easy glanced back at his friends. They urged him on.

"Change the channel."

"Zigzag has watched long enough."

"Why don't you just wait for a commercial?" X-Ray offered. "Then Easy can see what's happening on his channel. That all right with you, Zigzag?"

Zigzag's hand was still wrapped around Easy's, on top of the knob. "Okay," he agreed.

"That good for you, Easy?" X-Ray asked.

Easy looked around. For a second I thought he'd ease off, but then he said, "How the hell am I supposed to know when there's a commercial?"

He tried to turn the knob. Zigzag tightened his grip.

I could see the strain on their muscles and the tension on their faces. Easy's eyes began to water. Suddenly, he yelped like a dog and jerked his hand away.

"You're whacked out!" he exclaimed. "Look what he did to my hand!"

The channel knob was imprinted on Easy's palm. Cuts in his skin were shaped like little numbers.

Later, when a counselor asked Easy how he hurt his hand, he said, "I slammed the tent door on it."

That is what you should say whenever you get hurt in a fight, or even if someone hurts you accidentally. You never tattle.

We were always getting our hands or noses bashed in by those damn tent doors. It doesn't matter that there are no doors on the tents, just canvas flaps.

Later that night Zigzag lay on his cot, reading his *TV Guide.* He let out a deep sigh and said, "Man, too bad we don't get cable."

Tarantulas
(and Other Spiders)

This is what Mr. Sir says about tarantulas: "Their bark is worse than their bite." I think what Mr. Sir means is that tarantulas are a lot more scary-looking than they are dangerous. But Zigzag said he heard one bark.

If you see a tarantula crawling up your shirt, just brush it off. If it bites you, just wash the area with soap and water. It might be sore and red for a few days, but that's about it.

The general rule at Camp Green Lake is

the bigger the spider, the less deadly the venom. Tarantulas are big and hairy, about the size of a fist. They don't have to be deadly, because they scare everyone away. The smaller spiders need toxic venom to protect themselves. The most dangerous spiders at Camp Green Lake are the ones that are so small you can hardly see them.

Habitat: I don't know where tarantulas live. I just saw them crawling around, pretty much wherever they wanted. Smaller spiders make their homes under rocks and in the cracks in the concrete of the shower stalls.

Never pick up a rock with your bare hands. Use your shovel. X-Ray's eyesight wasn't very good, so before he would turn on the shower, he used to stomp around the area wearing just his shoes. It was kind of funny to watch, but we never laughed at X-Ray.

SURVIVAL TEST

3

You are filling your canteen at the spigot outside the shower wall. Someone says, "Hurry up, Snotface!" and shoves you from behind. The next morning when you wake up, the guy on the cot next to you tells you that you have a black eye. So how did you get the black eye?

A: A spider, living in the cracks by the spigot, bit you just below the eye.

B: When you were pushed, your face smashed against the water spigot.

C: You got the black eye fighting the guy who pushed you.

D: All of the above.

E: You don't have a black eye. It has been five months since your sheets were washed. That's dirt, grime, and mildew on your face.

ANSWER

The tent door slammed in your face.

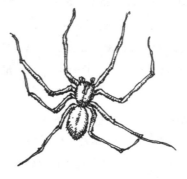

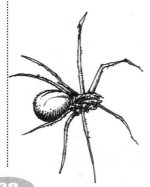

8

How to Dig a Hole

At the beginning of each day, Mr. Sir will tell you where to dig. Don't stop and ponder. Just get started. You want to get as much dug as you can before the sun rises.

The ground is hardest near the surface. Try to find a crack in the earth and wedge the shovel blade into it. Then stomp or jump on the back of the blade, driving the shovel into the ground. I'm a pretty heavy guy, so that helped, but it's not all about weight. Zero was the smallest guy in D tent, but he was our fastest digger.

Once you've loosened the dirt, try to get into a rhythm. Dig, scoop, toss. Dig, scoop, toss. One, two, three. Let your mind wander. Think about things you like. Things you don't like. Imagine that the dirt is Mr. Sir's face as you jab it with your shovel.

Your leg muscles are your strongest muscles, so use them. Don't put too much stress on your back. Bend your legs as you dig deep, then straighten them as you raise your shovel.

When your hole is finished, it will be five feet deep and five feet in diameter. Your shovel is your measuring stick. You must be able to lay your shovel flat across the bottom of your finished hole in any direction.

Allow yourself enough room. Be sure to toss the dirt far away from your hole, especially when you first start digging.

As your hole gets deeper, it will become harder to toss the dirt very far, so you will have to let it pile up near your hole. Be careful. There is nothing worse than having your dirt pile fall back into your hole. Always leave a clear space next to your hole.

This will allow you to climb in and out of your hole, and to measure the depth.

Don't ever toss your dirt into another digger's hole. Not by accident. Not as a joke. Never.

The water truck comes by every two hours, so ration your water accordingly. At about ten-thirty in the morning you'll get lunch: a sandwich, canned fruit, and a cookie. Don't open your sandwich to see what it is. You don't want to know. You probably wouldn't recognize it, anyway.

A supply truck comes to Camp Green Lake every two weeks, so if it's the day after the truck arrives, the bread and cookie might still be fresh. But once they're exposed to the dusty heat of the desert, they dry up pretty quickly.

The fruit comes in a sealed container. I recommend eating it very slowly, savoring every small bite. But everyone has his own way. Zigzag liked to eat whole slices of peaches. "I like the wet, slippery feeling as they slide down my throat."

Whatever.

The hardest time to dig is right after lunch. Your muscles will ache, and your hands will be blistered.

The last thing you'll want to do is climb back down into your hole and dig some more. You must. The hottest part of the day in Texas is between two and six o'clock. Just get off your dirt pile and back into rhythm. One, two, three. Dig, scoop, toss.

The first night, after digging your first hole, you'll be amazed how sore you are. It's not just your arms and legs that will hurt. My waist and groin hurt. I had swollen knees. My feet were blistered. My neck ached.

Over time your muscles will grow stronger. Your skin will toughen. But the hardest part about digging is not physical, it's mental.

You just can't let yourself think about how many holes you're going to have to dig, day after day, week after week, in the heat and the dust, month after month. Don't think about how many times you're going to have to stick your shovel in the earth and scoop out another shovelful of dirt.

You'll go crazy. Why do you think Barf Bag stepped on a rattlesnake? It wasn't an accident. He took off one shoe and one sock first.

I'm sorry if this section is getting a little long

and boring. The thing is, I know a lot about digging holes. But pay attention because now I'm going to give you my best advice, although you might find it hard to believe.

Try to dig a perfect hole.

I know that sounds really weird. Who cares if your hole is perfect? But if you're going to be out there six hours a day, you have to give yourself a purpose. You can either groan about how stupid it is to dig a hole, or you can tell yourself you're doing something important. You're digging the best hole anyone's ever dug.

It also helps physically. If you can make a perfect circle, exactly five feet in diameter and five feet deep, with sides that are perpendicular to the ground, you will have dug the absolute minimum amount of dirt required. No one's ever done that, not even Zero, but he's come close.

When you're done, stand over your hole. Take time to admire it, no matter how tired and sore you feel. You worked hard digging that hole, and you should take pride in a job well done.

And then spit in it. Because, after all, it's just a stupid hole, and you are better than that.

9

The Road to Freedom

It took me over eight hours to get to Camp Green Lake in the Texas Youth Authority bus. The last three hours of the trip were on the same long, straight road. The road was paved at first, but the pavement seemed to crumble away until it was nothing but a dusty dirt road. Outside the dirty windows there was nothing but miles and miles of brush and weeds. Then, as we got closer to Camp Green Lake, all I saw were holes and dirt piles.

This is the only road in and out of Camp

Green Lake. Every two weeks a supply truck rumbles into the camp compound, bringing everything from five-gallon cans of peas to a new jigsaw puzzle for the Warden.

Most of the time, you forget the road is even there. Every once in a while, when you're out there digging, you'll notice the road cutting right through the sea of holes. Something about it seems unreal. If you stare at it long enough, it seems to rise up and float just above the holes.

Somewhere at the other end are all the things that aren't at Camp Green Lake: beds with clean sheets; toilets that flush; food that doesn't come from a can. Girls. Girls with clean hair. Girls in bikinis. Girls on TV. Girls talking together as they walk down the school hallway. Girls concentrating in algebra class, trying so hard to get a good grade, with no idea of how they made me feel inside.

Don't get me wrong. I'm not some kind of sex maniac or anything. Back at school, I was fat and unpopular. Girls ignored me. But still, after working, sleeping, and eating with a group of sweaty guys in orange suits day in and day out, I couldn't help thinking about all the girls at the other end of that road. The way they walked. The way they talked. Even the way they seemed to look right through me as if I was invisible.

And if that was how I felt, it was probably ten times worse for the other guys who had girlfriends back home. Or, if not girlfriends, at least girls who would talk to them.

But you can't think about what's at the other end of the road. The road is too long.

We were out there one day, digging not too far from the road. Magnet just kept stopping and staring. It was like he was hypnotized. I was usually the slowest digger, but when the lunch break came, my hole was a foot deeper than Magnet's.

"Man, you got to snap out of it," X-Ray warned him. "You'll be out here all day."

"I'm leaving this place," Magnet declared.

"There's only one way out of here," X-Ray said.

"Down that road," said Magnet.

"In a coffin," said X-Ray.

Magnet just kept staring down the road. "Next time the supply truck comes and goes," he said, "I'll jump on the back bumper and ride all the way to San Antonio."

"Supply truck's coming today," said Zigzag. "It's been two weeks."

Somehow, Zigzag always knew the day of the week. Maybe it had something to do with his TV schedule.

"You ain't goin' nowhere," said X-Ray.

We heard the truck before we saw it: a low rumble way off in the distance. Then the dust cloud appeared just above the horizon. Fifteen minutes later the truck lumbered by.

Magnet climbed out of his hole.

"How you gonna jump on a moving truck?" Squid asked.

"I'm gonna dig a ditch across the road," he said. "The truck'll have to slow down."

I pointed out that the truck driver might get suspicious, since the ditch wasn't there when he drove in.

"It's a long, old road," said Magnet. "You think the driver remembers every pothole?"

Armpit seemed especially worried. "The truck will go really fast. How are you going to be able to stand on the bumper of a fast-moving truck for hundreds of miles?"

Magnet smiled. "I'm a human magnet," he said. "Besides, they probably leave the truck unlatched. I'll just slip inside."

"You ain't goin' nowhere," said X-Ray.

"Just watch me," said Magnet, and taking his shovel, he headed for the road.

I did watch him, for a while. As I dug my hole, I could see him digging his ditch. I felt like a part of me was out there digging with him.

I knew the Warden would punish all of us. If nothing else, we'd have to dig Magnet's hole. But I didn't worry about that for the moment. If Magnet could get away, it was like a part of me would be free, too.

I wasn't worried about Mr. Sir or Mr. Pendanski coming by. I knew they were busy with the supply truck. The counselors always took the best stuff for themselves.

After a while, I couldn't see Magnet anymore. He must have finished the ditch and been hiding behind a dirt pile nearby.

I was about chest high in my hole when the truck came barreling down the road. A huge dust cloud trailed behind it. We climbed out of our holes to watch.

The truck suddenly braked sharply, and I heard Zero whisper, "All right." I felt really nervous, like I was the one about to jump on the back.

But I couldn't see what happened. The dust cloud caught up with and encircled the braking truck as it bounced over the ditch. Then the truck picked up speed and thundered off, the cloud of dust swirling behind it.

"Anyone see him?" asked Armpit.

"Yeah, he jumped on the back and stuck to it like a magnet on a refrigerator," said Zigzag.

"Yeah, well just 'cause Zigzag sees something doesn't mean it's there," said X-Ray.

"And just because you don't see something doesn't mean it's not there," said Zigzag.

I returned to my hole but continued to watch the truck until it disappeared over the horizon. I finished digging, took my shower, then hung out in the Wreck Room until dinner. Nobody spoke about

Magnet, in case the Warden was listening, but we were all thinking about him.

He showed up halfway through dinner. He just walked into the mess hall, still in his sweaty uniform, got his tray of food, and plopped down at our table. The only thing he said was "Pass the ketchup."

We stared at him.

"Good to see you, buddy," said X-Ray. "Didn't you hear him, Squid? Give the man some ketchup."

SURVIVAL TEST

What happened to Magnet?

A: He hid behind a dirt pile and watched the truck go by, too scared to try to jump on it. Ashamed, he waited until we all returned to the camp compound, then finished digging his hole.

B: He jumped on the back bumper but immediately fell off. He lay in the road, defeated, as he watched the truck drive away. Bruised and ashamed, he waited until we all finished digging, then returned to his hole.

C: He jumped on the back bumper and had ridden for about a mile when suddenly the truck hit a bump in the road and he fell off, nearly killing himself. He limped back down the road, then finished digging his hole.

D: He jumped on the back bumper and held on to the latch. As the truck picked up speed, he got more and more scared. Before the truck reached an unsafe speed, he jumped off, hit the road hard, then bounced and rolled down the road. He lay there awhile, waiting for someone to come get him. When no one did, he pulled himself to his feet, limped back down the road, and finished digging his hole.

E: He jumped on the back bumper, opened the latch, and slipped inside, only to find workers playing cards. He was taken to Mr. Pendanski, who lectured him, then to Mr. Sir, who yelled at him, then to the Warden, who punished him, and then he had to finish digging his hole.

ANSWER

I don't know. I'm as curious as you are, but I never found out. If Magnet had wanted to tell us, he would have. The important thing is this: If you're going to survive Camp Green Lake, you just can't ask too many questions.

10

Rattlesnakes

Types of rattlesnakes: It may be helpful for you to know the different kinds of rattlesnakes found at Camp Green Lake and to be able to recognize each type by its color and distinct markings. Unfortunately, I can't help you there. When it comes to rattlesnakes, I'm basically a blubbering idiot. All I ever notice are the two ends, the rattle and the mouth. I can't tell you much about the middle.

I think they're pretty much the color of sand, which is pretty much the color of everything else at Camp Green Lake. I've heard Mr. Pendanski refer to one as a diamondback, so it's a good bet it has diamond markings on its back.

Another type is the sidewinder, which I can recognize not by its markings but by the way it moves. When a sidewinder is chasing after you, it doesn't keep its body in a straight line. Instead, it looks like a series of S curves, which slither very rapidly with

a wavelike motion. I wish I could give you a better description, but I don't have eyes in the back of my head.

The coiled rattlesnake: Most rattlesnakes I saw were in a coil. This is the snake's most dangerous position, because of how quickly it can become uncoiled. Usually, the snake will see you before you see it. That's good. If you saw it first, you might already be too close.

When the snake sees you, its tail will begin to rattle. You can see the rattle sticking straight up from somewhere in the middle of the coil. The rattles are four to six inches long. Imagine trying to shake a baby's rattle as fast as you can for as long as you can. Your arm would get tired after thirty seconds. The snake's tail rattles much faster, about ten rattles per second, and it doesn't seem to get tired. It would be interesting to know how long a rattlesnake can keep on rattling, but that would require sticking around.

Also rising up from the coil will be the head. As you circle around a coiled snake, the raised head will turn 360 degrees, watching you; the snake's mouth will be open, its forked tongue darting in and out between two large fangs.

Even a dead rattlesnake can bite you. Rattlesnakes are not the most intelligent creatures on the planet. If their sensors detect danger, they strike. It's just a reflex. They don't think about it. If a rattlesnake has been recently killed, some of its nerve endings may still be working. If you try to pick up a dead rattle-snake, it may still bite you, as a reflex.

What to do if you are bitten by a rattlesnake: Don't panic. The good news is that one way or another, you are about to leave Camp Green Lake.

"What do you think Barf Bag is doing right now?"

That question was asked my first night in D tent. Barf Bag had stepped on a rattlesnake. I was his replacement.

"I bet he's lying in a hospital bed, watching television," said Zigzag.

"On clean sheets," said Armpit.

"Drinking milk shakes through a straw," said Squid.

"Beautiful nurses come by every fifteen minutes," said Magnet. "And gently pat his head with cool washcloths."

"Or else, he's dead," said X-Ray.

We must have had a hundred similar conversations during my time at the camp. Whenever anyone was feeling lonely or desperate, he'd ask, "What do you think Barf Bag's doing right now?" And then we'd all try to imagine. I guess it helped.

I don't recommend taking Barf Bag's approach. If a rattler bites you, you will need medical treatment as soon as possible. If someone is coming for you, you should lie down, keeping the snakebite below your heart. If you have to go back to camp, take it slow and easy.

The nearest hospital to Camp Green Lake is over a hundred miles away; however, they have a helicopter. It's about an hour-and-a-half trip each way. In the meantime, the Warden keeps a supply of antivenin.

Antivenin is made from rattlesnake venom. Scientists inject tiny doses of snake venom into a horse until the horse becomes immune. The antivenin is then derived from the horse's blood.

Mr. Sir sometimes catches rattlesnakes and

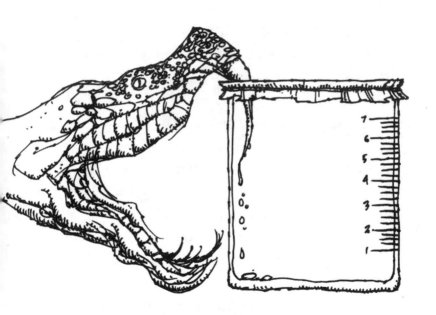

brings them to the Warden. The Warden extracts the venom herself. X-Ray watched her do it one time.

With one hand, she held the live rattlesnake

right behind its head. In her other hand, she held a beaker with a thin piece of rubber stretched over it. She then brought the beaker toward the snake. The snake struck at it. Its fangs pierced the rubber cover, and venom squirted into the beaker.

The Warden showed X-Ray the snake's venom glands, which were located right behind its eyes. She gently stroked the glands, causing more venom to fill the beaker.

"It was really cool," he told us.

I don't know if the Warden used any of this venom to make antivenin. I think it was mainly used for cosmetics.

11

Twitch

Twitch did everything wrong. He is a good example of how not to survive. He was Zero's replacement.

When he was brought to D tent, he immediately began poking through all the crates. "What's this for?" he kept asking as he touched all our stuff. "March 22, 1998? I think you can throw this away." He tossed the *TV Guide* on the floor. "Whose octopus?"

The tent door slammed in his face.

Twitch's biggest problem was that he had too much nervous energy. He couldn't sit still. X-Ray named him Twitch because some part of his body was always twitching.

We tested him. "See if you can sit perfectly still for five minutes," Armpit challenged. "No moving."

Twitch sat on his cot, Zero's cot, and tried not to move a muscle.

Nobody had a watch, but Zigzag said he'd count to five hundred. "One Mississippi, two Mississippi . . ."

If Zero had still been there, he might have pointed out that Zigzag should count to three hundred. Zero was good at math, but knowing Zero, he probably wouldn't have said anything. Of course if Zero had still been there, then Twitch wouldn't have been.

". . . Twenty-two Mississippi. Twenty-three Mississippi."

The muscles on Twitch's face jumped and fluttered. His eyes blinked constantly. I thought I saw his ear wiggle. "I have a cousin who lives in McGehee, Arkansas," he suddenly blurted out. "We'd go and drive four-wheelers down by the Mississippi River."

"Shhh," Armpit whispered.

Twitch really tried. He just couldn't do it. Zigzag

was at seventy-three Mississippi when Twitch abruptly stood up and said he'd had enough.

Magnet said he thought that instead of blood, Twitch had coffee in his veins.

"I guess I'm a little nervous," Twitch admitted.

"Seventy-three seconds," said Zigzag. "He couldn't even last a minute."

You should never do anything fast at Camp Green Lake. Walk, don't run. Even if a sidewinder is coming after you, you just walk quickly out of the way. Always look where you're going. The last thing you want to do is run away from a rattlesnake and into a yellow-spotted lizard.

Twitch did everything way too fast. He moved in quick, jerky steps and was always looking from side to side, never in front of him. He even talked fast.

"What's your deal, Zigzag? Anyone ever tell you, you look kind of weird? You should do something with your hair, man, if you know what I mean. So, what's the worst crime anyone did here? Any murderers?"

"Quit bumping your gums," X-Ray said, which was his way of telling Twitch to shut up.

"Bumping my gums, that's a good one. I'll have to remember that. So what happened to Zero?"

"You ask too many questions," I told him.

"I just want to know what happened. Why are you so touchy?"

I didn't feel like talking about it. Zero had become my best friend, and what happened to him had been my fault.

Twitch ate fast, too. You should always eat slowly. It's not about having good manners. You don't know what you're eating, and you may have to suddenly spit something out.

He talked while he ate. "Five-foot holes. That's a lotta dirt. Whew! I bet you get tired. How long does that take? About an hour?"

"About," I said.

I could have told him the truth, but it didn't matter. Twitch asked lots of questions but never stopped to listen to an answer.

He tossed and turned all night in bed. I know. I was up all night worrying about Zero. But when the horn blew the next morning, Twitch jumped out of bed, ready to go.

"Man, look at all the stars. That's the Big Dipper. I never saw this many stars in Plano."

I tried to tell him he was better off keeping his eyes on the ground, but he didn't listen.

"That's the Little Dipper. Hey, Armpit, what sign are you?"

"This is my sign," Armpit said, and gave him the finger.

"Don't talk so much," Magnet said. "You got to save your strength."

"I never get tired," said Twitch.

"Well, you're making me tired just listening to you," said X-Ray.

Out at the digging area, Mr. Sir gave Twitch the usual instructions. "You're not finished until your hole is as deep and as wide as your shovel. If you dig up anything unusual, you're to report it to me or Mr. Pendanski. The water truck will—"

Twitch didn't have the patience to listen. "Quit bumping your gums," he said, "and show me where I'm supposed to dig."

We all stopped and stared. I don't think I have to tell you that you don't talk to Mr. Sir that way.

But Mr. Sir just smiled, then made an X in the dirt with the heel of his boot. "Right here," he said.

I guess he knew he didn't have to do anything to Twitch. Twitch would soon be suffering enough.

As soon as Mr. Sir stepped away, Twitch's shovel cut through the X and the dirt was flying. I'd never seen anyone dig so fast. Zero had been a fast digger, but it was never about speed. It was his steadiness that made him fast. His movements were smooth. He kept his rhythm and never wavered.

Twitch dug in short, quick strokes. He was all arms and back. He'd stop and take long gulps of water, and even pour some water on his head.

I tried to tell him he had to save his water, but he wouldn't listen. "Talk to me when your hole is as deep as mine!"

He was right about that. His hole was twice as deep as mine was. He scooped up another shovelful of dirt and tossed it right where Armpit was digging.

Armpit walked over to Twitch and threw a

handful of dirt in his face. "Your dirt landed in my hole." Then he walked back to his hole.

"What's his problem?" Twitch asked, wiping the dirt from his eye. He didn't realize he'd gotten off easy. I hoped, for his sake, no more of his dirt would land in Armpit's hole.

I didn't have to worry. It was right about then that Twitch started wearing down. His shovel got slower, and slower, and then, for the first time since he got to Camp Green Lake, Twitch stopped twitching.

Then the moaning and groaning started. "My hands hurt. Ahggh. I can't hold the shovel." His voice was raspy, and all kinds of strange sounds came out of him. "Ahgha. Oy-yah. Anybody got any water they don't want? Uhnnhhk. Caveman, can I have some of your water?"

Yeah, right.

"First hole's the hardest," I told him.

That was a lie. The second hole is a lot harder. You're tired and sore before you even crawl out of bed.

The water truck came an hour later. Twitch used his last ounce of strength to drag himself out of his hole and scramble to the front of the line. But that isn't how things are done at Camp Green Lake. You have to earn your place in line.

X-Ray was always first, followed by Armpit, Squid, Zigzag, Magnet, and then me. I didn't get in line that day, so Twitch took my place.

I wish I could tell you if and how Twitch made it through the day, and if he survived Camp Green Lake, but I left the camp abruptly after the arrival of the water truck and went out searching for Zero. One of the last things I heard Twitch say was "Hey, check out this awesome lizard!"

12

Yellow-Spotted Lizards

How to recognize a yellow-spotted lizard: You'll hardly see the yellow spots. The first things you'll notice are the huge red eyes, then the sharp black teeth, and then the long white tongue. I don't know what makes the eleven small yellow spots on the lizard's back so special. Perhaps there's another type of lizard with red eyes, black teeth, and a ten-inch tongue that doesn't have yellow spots.

If you see a yellow-spotted lizard, forget about everything else I've

told you and just run. Don't look where you're going. Go! Scream if you want.

The yellow-spotted lizard's venom is ten times more toxic than rattlesnake venom, and there is no antivenin. The lizards have powerful legs, and unlike scorpions, they know how to use them.

Habitat: Holes, five feet deep, five feet in diameter.

What to do if you are bitten by a yellow-spotted lizard: If there is something you wanted to do in your life before you died, now's the time to do it.

SURVIVAL TEST

You have just stolen Mr. Sir's water truck and are speeding away across the digging area. You should:

A: Fasten your seat belt.

B: Stop. Bang your head against the steering wheel several times and repeat, "What have I done? What have I done?"

C: Return to Mr. Sir and say, "The brakes are fine, but you'll need to adjust the carburetor."

D: Whatever. It doesn't matter.

E: *Look out!!!*

ANSWER

D is the correct answer. There are only two possible explanations for your situation. Either you are dreaming, or you've been bitten by a yellow-spotted lizard and you wanted to drive a truck before you died. In either case, it doesn't matter what you do.

13

X-Ray and the B-Tent Boys

You might say X-Ray survived too well.

From the very beginning, when I was first taken to D tent, it was obvious who was the leader. It wasn't Armpit or Squid, the two toughest guys in the tent. It was X-Ray, a skinny kid who wore thick glasses that were so dirty he needed X-ray vision just to see out of them.

His secret was his confidence and his smile. He was always cool, even in the heat of Green Lake. When he smiled, it made you feel that everything would be all right.

He didn't need to be tough. He had Armpit and Squid by his side. They would do his dirty work for him if necessary, but it was hardly ever necessary. It seemed everyone wanted to stay on X-Ray's good side.

Part of it was survival. I knew that if I was going to survive Camp Green Lake, I couldn't have X-Ray mad at me. But it was more than that. When I did something for him, he would smile his great smile, look me right in the eye, and say, "Thanks, Caveman. You're a good guy." He made me feel cool and confident, too.

He would do things for you—get you an extra piece of bread or a clean pair of socks. Of course, X-Ray never did anything for anybody unless he got something for himself, too. Like the time he saved Zigzag from the B-tent boys and got everyone in D tent an extra carton of orange juice.

The B-tent boys were a couple of years older than us, and they were some of the meanest and toughest guys in camp. One of them was named Thlump, and he was even crazier than Zigzag. I think at one time his name was The Lump, but it turned into one word.

There was a boom box in the Wreck Room. It was a combination radio, cassette player, and CD player, but we were out of range of any radio station, and we didn't have any cassettes. Thlump owned the only CD in camp. It was the first CD put out by the Backstreet Boys. Now, I had always thought only twelve-year-old girls liked the Backstreet Boys, but this was Thlump's lifeline.

Don't get me wrong. I've got nothing against the Backstreet Boys. I'm sure lots of people like their music, but after you've heard the same CD over and over and over again, day after day after day, it becomes a kind of torture. There was one song, "If You Want It to Be Good Girl (Get Yourself a Bad Boy)," which he'd sometimes play five times in a row, while he and his buddies sang along with the chorus.

That was the song that was playing when suddenly Zigzag got up from the floor, walked over to them, and said, "You mind turning that down? I'm trying to watch *Ally McBeal*."

About that time, the chorus kicked in and they

all started singing along. So Ziggy reached over and turned off the music. The entire room became instantly quiet, not just the Backstreet Boys.

Thlump wrapped his big hand over Zigzag's face and pressed his head against the wall. "You're dead," he whispered.

X-Ray instantly eased himself between Thlump and two of his goons. "Hey, guys," he said calmly.

"Stay away, X-Ray," Thlump warned. "I don't want to hurt you, too."

X-Ray showed no sign of fear. "How would you like some new tunes?" he asked.

Thlump still held Zigzag. "You're loonier than your friend," he said.

"What kinda new tunes?" asked one of the goons.

"What do you want?" X-Ray asked.

Thlump let go of Zigzag. "How you gonna get new tunes way out here?"

"I got connections," said X-Ray. "But it's going to cost you."

"It's going to cost *me*?" asked Thlump. "You're lucky I don't kill you and your friend."

"A week's worth of orange juice," X-Ray said. "From you and everyone in B tent."

The B-tenters looked at each other, then back at X-Ray.

"Can you get the Backstreet Boys' second CD?" Thlump asked.

Everyone in the Wreck Room groaned.

X-Ray smiled.

I didn't know how he did it, but two days later X-Ray brought them their CD, and for the next three days, we all got an extra carton of orange juice. It was supposed to be for a week, but after three days, X-Ray told the B-tenters they didn't have to pay anymore. I was disappointed, but who was I to complain? At least I got extra orange juice for a few days, and got to hear some new music, sort of.

Of course we didn't get the extra orange juice for nothing. We each had to give X-Ray half a piece of bread, but it was still a great deal for us.

I saw X-Ray last week. He lives in Lubbock. "He's in his room doing his homework," his mother told me, then pointed the way. "And remind him I'm still waiting for him to take out the garbage."

X-Ray's door was open. I could see him at his desk, which was covered with books and paper. He mumbled something about Angle C.

"X-Ray," I said.

He turned. "Caveman! Good to see you."

His face looked different. It wasn't just that his glasses were clean. He seemed hassled and worn out. Despite the air-conditioning, beads of sweat had collected on his forehead.

I told him I was writing a survival guide to Camp Green Lake and then asked him how he managed to get the new CD for the B-Tent Boys.

He smiled, and for a second he looked like his old self again. "I went to Pendanski," he said. "Asked him what kind of music he liked."

"The Backstreet Boys?" I asked.

X-Ray laughed. "Nah, he'd never heard of them. It was someone ancient and boring. The Rolling Rocks, I think. But I told him they were my favorite group, too. He started naming songs I'd never heard of, and I'd say stuff like 'Rock on' and 'Awesome licks.' Made him feel like he was the coolest cat in the state of Texas."

I could imagine.

X-Ray's mother shouted to him from another room. "Rex, you still haven't taken out the garbage!"

"I got a friend here!" X-Ray shouted back, then continued his story. "So anyway, I told Pendanski, for the sake of camp morale, we should get some new music for the Wreck Room. Except I made him feel like it was his idea."

X-Ray's mother opened the door. She was skinny and wore glasses, too. "I'm not going to tell you again," she said. "And you know the rules about having friends over on a school night."

"He's writing a book about Camp Green Lake," said X-Ray. " I'm going to be in it."

His mother scowled at me. "I'm sorry, but I really

don't want Rex associating with . . ." She paused, unsure of how to put it, but I got the idea.

She turned to X-Ray. "Have you finished your homework?"

"I'll do it!"

"Don't snap at me," his mother warned, then walked out.

He quickly finished his story. Mr. Pendanski was good at computers, so they had no trouble downloading the music off the Internet and burning it on a CD. X-Ray convinced him that the other guys wouldn't appreciate the Rolling Rocks, so they chose the Backstreet Boys instead.

X-Ray looked back down at his homework. "Man, who cares what angles are congruent?"

I shrugged.

"We were supposed to get orange juice for a week," I said. "How come you let them off the hook after just three days?"

"They woulda quit paying anyway," X-Ray said. "This way they thought I was doing them a favor." He laughed. "They owed me."

It was good to see his cool, confident smile again.

"Man, those were the good old days," he said. Then he shook his head and sighed. "Sorry, you got to go. Homework."

On my way outside, I took out the garbage for him.

SURVIVAL TEST

What is your name?

A: Barf Bag

B: Snotface

C: Thworm

D: David Divad

E: Hannah

ANSWER

I think this was an easy question, especially if your name happened to be one of the five choices given. Even if it wasn't, you should have gotten the correct answer, but only you know your own name. You're on the honor system.

Whatever your name is, after you've been at Camp Green Lake awhile, you'll be given a new name. Chances are it will be something weird or gross. That's good. No matter how weird a name you get, you should be glad. It means you've been accepted. If you've been there two weeks and they still call you Scott, or Chris, or Rebecca, you've been doing something wrong, and you better figure out what it is.

If you're lucky, your new name will get a nickname. In my group, Squid was sometimes called Squidly. Zigzag was also called Zig or Ziggy. X-Ray was X. Armpit was also just plain Pit. I was either Caveman or the Caveman.

But don't forget who you really are. And I'm not talking about your so-called real name. All names are made up by someone else, even the one your parents gave you.

You know who you really are. When you're alone at night, looking up at the stars, or maybe lying in your bed in total darkness, you know that nameless person inside you.

Your life is about to be ripped apart. You will be turned into a digging machine. Your muscles will toughen. So will your heart and soul. That's necessary for your survival. But don't lose touch with that person deep inside you, or else you won't really have survived at all.

APPENDIX

These are the people I met at Camp Green Lake. You will deal with a whole new set of fellow campers, but the lessons you learned in this survival guide should apply. The names may change, but human nature doesn't.

MR. SIR: Before Camp Green Lake, it is believed he sold stolen property out of the back room of a bar in El

Paso. He got wind of an upcoming police raid and skipped town, driving a motorcycle (probably stolen) across the Texas desert. He met the Warden, who hired him to run the camp. Police investigators found no evidence linking him with any crime. The motorcycle can't be found, no doubt buried in a hole.

MR. PENDANSKI: He was kicked out of the University of Texas for cheating. He had hacked into the central computer and changed grades. He also downloaded copies of the questions that would be on final exams and sold them to other students. The Warden hired him for his computer skills.

ARMPIT: Despite his parents' pleas, he hung around with the wrong crowd and got in a fight. "I didn't start the fight, but I sure the hell finished it." He sent two boys to the hospital and got himself sent to Camp Green Lake. Since being released, he has stayed out of trouble. He avoids violence and, despite the coaches' pleas, refuses to join his high school football team in Austin.

ZIGZAG: Was setting fire to pieces of Styrofoam in the schoolyard when the flames got out of control and destroyed a portable classroom. "I didn't do it on purpose. I just like to watch things burn." Since being released, he hasn't watched much television. "There's nothing good on anymore."

SQUID: When Squid was three years old, his father

went out "to buy some ice cream" and never returned. His mother is an alcoholic. Squid used to skip school and break into homes in his neighborhood, stealing mostly loose change and cans

of soda. He now lives with his cousins in Missouri. He is two years behind in school, but he is working hard and hopes to go to college someday and study marine biology.

MAGNET: Shoplifting, and I'm not talking about stealing a candy bar from 7-Eleven. After he was arrested,

the police found over five thousand dollars' worth of stolen property in his bedroom. "It's all in your attitude. I once walked out of a Wal-Mart carrying a DVD player and a fax machine, and they

held the door open for me." He was arrested when he tried to "rescue" a puppy from a cage in a pet store. He now volunteers once a week at the Humane Society in San Antonio.

X-RAY: Sold drugs, though he never used any himself. "If not me, they would have gotten their stuff from someone else, right?" He would have faced a much longer prison term, but it turned out the drugs were not what they appeared to be. The bags of white powder contained only chopped-up aspirin. However, it was still illegal to sell bags of aspirin without a pharmaceutical license. X-Ray is currently attending high school, which he claims is much harder than Camp Green Lake.

 TWITCH: When Camp Green Lake was initially closed, he was transferred to a special home for troubled youths in Houston. There he learned to play the guitar. He now has his own band called the Constant Fidgeters.

 BARF BAG: He made a full recovery. Believing he would be sent back to Camp Green Lake, he ran away from the hospital. He didn't realize that his time in the hospital counted as time served in prison, and that he had, in fact, completed his sentence. His current whereabouts are unknown. If you see him, please tell him it's safe to go home.

ZERO: For privacy reasons, no information is available.

CAVEMAN: (me) It's funny. The Warden didn't care about

building character. I wrote this survival guide because Camp Green Lake was such a miserable place. And yet, when I think about it, I have to admit I feel a lot better about myself now than I did before I went there. I'm full of self-confidence. I'm in good physical shape. Kids don't bully me. I have friends. Most important, I like who I am. I didn't before.

My best friend also goes to my high school. He never had any formal education, but with the help of tutoring, he's doing real well, especially at math. He doesn't talk much and mostly keeps to himself, but still everyone likes him. I won't say his name because he values his privacy.

I sort of have a girlfriend, too—well, not really a girlfriend, I mean, I like her, and I'm pretty sure she likes me. She smiles at me a lot, and she's just so easy to talk to, but I don't know, she's such a kind and warmhearted person, she's probably like that with everyone. Sometimes she calls me Caveman, with just a little bit of a tease in her voice. I like saying her name, too. It's—well, I better not mention her name, because if it turns out she doesn't like me, this would really be embarrassing. Maybe I'm not quite as self-confident as I said I was.

I don't complain. I don't ask too many questions. I try to make the right choices. And I'm still trying to dig the perfect hole.